three-minute tales

MY FARMYARD TREASURY

p

This Book Belongs To

This is a Parragon book
This edition published in 2002

Parragon
Queen Street House, 4 Queen Street,
Bath, BA1 1HE, UK

Produced by The Templar Company plc
Pippbrook Mill, London Road, Dorking,
Surrey, RH4 1JE, UK

Printed and bound in China
ISBN 0 75258 759 5

.three-minute tales.
MY FARMYARD TREASURY

Written by Emily Fortune • Illustrated by Stephanie Boey and Mario Capaldi

CONTENTS

LAMB'S TALE

One sunny day, Lamb was playing in the field with

his best friends, Duck, Hen and Piglet.

"Let's play 'What's the time, Mr Wolf?'" said Hen.

"Great!" said Duck. "Who wants to be Mr Wolf?"

"Me! Me! Me!" said Lamb, bouncing up and down.

It was his favourite game.

He skipped to the end of the field and turned his back,

while the others stood behind him in a line.

"What's the time, Mr Wolf?" called Duck.

"One o'clock!" bleated Lamb.

The others took a step forward.

"What's the time, Mr Wolf?" called Hen.

"Two o'clock!" shouted Lamb.

They stepped closer, giggling nervously.

"What's the time, Mr Wolf?" called Piglet.

"Three o'clock!" yelled Lamb, trying to sound

scary, as the others crept closer still.

"What's the time, Mr Wolf?" asked Duck.

Lamb turned around. He was about to shout 'DINNERTIME!' and start chasing after his friends. But instead he bleated, "Wolf! Wolf!" Piglet, Hen and Duck looked at Lamb in surprise. "That's not right, Lamb," said Duck. "You're supposed to say 'Dinnertime!' and then try to catch us as we all run away."

"But there IS a wolf," said Lamb, his eyes wide with

alarm, "and it really IS his dinnertime!"

Lamb's friends looked at him crossly.

"Lamb, you're spoiling the game," Duck complained.

"Stop trying to scare us!"

"Look!" Lamb bleated pointing behind them.

Duck, Hen and Piglet turned and looked over their shoulders. Lamb was right — there really was a wolf! The four animals raced back to the farmyard as fast as their legs would carry them. "Tomorrow," said Lamb, "let's play hopscotch." And everyone agreed.

SPRING LAMB

Spring Lamb was the bounciest lamb on the farm –
all the other animals said so. The other lambs tried
hard to jump as high as she did, but nobody could.
"Spring Lamb, you're so bouncy!" everyone cried
and Spring Lamb felt so pleased with herself that
she started to show off!

"Look at me!" she called to her friends. "I'm going to jump right over that big, high gate!" "Don't be silly," said Shep the Sheepdog, looking worried. "It's far too high for a small lamb like you to jump."

"Nonsense," said Spring Lamb, bouncing over to the gate. "I'm the best jumper in the world!" Now she was close to it, the gate did look very high. But Spring Lamb wanted to impress everyone. She just HAD to jump it now!

Spring Lamb ran and took a great leap —up...up...up!
But not up enough. Poor Spring Lamb was stuck
with her little woolly head on one side of the gate, and
her little woolly bottom on the other!
Luckily, Shep came to her rescue.
"You were right, after all, Shep," said Spring Lamb.
"But I'm not too small to jump over you!"
And that's just what she did!

LOST LAMB

Little Lamb was forever wandering off – after all,
the world was such an exciting place to explore!
"Little Lamb," said her mummy, "you must stay
where I can see you. Otherwise you might get lost
or get into trouble." But Little Lamb wasn't
listening. She was far too busy chasing rabbits
or playing with the frogs by the stream.

One day, Little Lamb spotted a big blue dragonfly hovering over the water. She chased after it, skipping across a stone bridge to the other side of the stream, but she soon lost sight of it. And when she looked round, she couldn't see her mummy anywhere either.

"Baa-a-a!" bleated Little Lamb, suddenly feeling
lost and alone. "Where are you, Mummy?"
Then in the distance she heard her mummy calling:
"Baa-a-a! Where are you, Little Lamb?"
Little Lamb ran towards her mummy's voice.

As she crossed the little stone bridge, she looked over the side. Her mummy was stuck in the stream with her foot caught in the stones. Quickly, Little Lamb called to her friends, and together they pulled her mummy free. Now Little Lamb was a bit wet and soggy, but at least she wasn't lost any more.

"I'll never wander away again, Mummy," she said.

"Just look at the trouble you get into without me!"

WOOLLY LAMB

It was a lovely sunny day in spring. Bees were
buzzing, and birds were singing. Everyone was
happy and busy, all except Woolly Lamb.
"I'm far too hot!" she complained, miserably.
"But it's such a beautiful spring day,"
said Mouse, scurrying past.
"It's alright for you," grumbled Woolly Lamb, "you
don't have to wear this warm, woolly coat!"

Just then, Bluebird perched beside Woolly Lamb. "Your wool would make a lovely soft lining for my nest, ready for my eggs to hatch in," she chirped. "Please help yourself," said Woolly Lamb. "I've got far too much!" So Bluebird loaded up her beak with soft wool, and flew away happily.

A little later, Mouse came by.
"Your wool would make a lovely warm bed
for my babies," she sighed.
"Take as much as you like," said Woolly Lamb.
"I've got plenty." So Mouse took a bundle
and ran away happily to her home.

Later, Bluebird showed Woolly Lamb three eggs snuggled into the soft wool lining her warm nest. Woolly Lamb felt proud to have helped. And when she saw four sleepy baby mice tucked up in the cosy bed Mouse had made, she felt prouder still. "My woolly coat does make a nice warm blanket," she said, sniffing the cool night air. "I guess I'm lucky to be such a woolly little lamb, after all!"

DANNY DUCKLING IN TROUBLE

"Stay still so I can count!" quacked Mummy Duck crossly, as the little ducklings splashed about. "Just as I thought, Danny's missing again. We'd better go and look for him!" It was the third time that week Danny Duckling had got lost. He liked to swim at the end of the line and often got left behind. But this time he was in trouble...

Earlier that day, Danny had been following along through the reeds when his foot caught in something beneath the water.

"Bother!" he quacked as he tried to pull it free.

He ducked into the water and saw that his foot was tangled in an old fishing net held fast in the mud. "Help!" he cried to the others, but they were already too far away to hear.

The more Danny struggled, the tighter the net gripped his foot. "Help!" he quacked, flapping his fluffy little wings. Luckily, Freya Frog heard his cries and dived under the water to try and free him, but it was no use. "I'll go and get help," she said, swimming off. "Hurry!" Danny called after her. The tide was coming in and the river was rising fast!

By the time Freya returned with Wally Water Rat, the water was covering Danny's back. "I'm going to be pulled under!" cried Danny. "Don't worry," said Wally. "We'll save you!" In no time at all, Wally's sharp teeth nibbled through the net,

and Danny bobbed back to the surface
just as his mummy appeared.
"Thank goodness you're safe," said Mummy.
"But from now on swim at the front of the
line." And that is just what Danny did.

ALL AT SEA!

It was a lovely spring day when Dippy Duckling

peeked out of her warm nest at the shimmering

river. How cool and inviting the water looked.

Soon she was swimming along happily, calling

out to all the animals that lived on the riverbank

as she went by. She didn't realise how fast or

how far the current was carrying her

as she swept along past forests and fields.

As Dippy floated on enjoying the warm sun on her back Sally Seagull flew by squawking loudly. "I've never seen a bird like that on the river before," thought Dippy, in surprise.

Then just as she came round a great bend in the river she saw the wide shining ocean spread out in front of her! Dippy began to shake with terror — she was going to be swept out to sea!

She started to paddle furiously against the tide, but it was no use. The current was too strong.

Just then, a friendly face popped up nearby. It was Ollie Otter. He was very surprised to find Dippy so far from home. "Climb on my back," he said. Soon his strong legs were pulling them back up the river and safely home.

"Thank you, Ollie," said Dippy. "Without you, I'd be all at sea!"

FOREVER FRIENDS

Daisy Duckling had lots of friends but her best
friend of all was Cindy Cygnet. Every day they
played together, chasing each other through
the reeds. "When I grow up, I'll be a beautiful
swan like my mummy!" said Cindy.
"And I'll be a dull little brown duck," said Daisy.
She worried that Cindy would only want to play
with her pretty swan friends when she grew up.

Then one day, they were playing hide and seek
when something dreadful happened.
While Daisy hid amongst some large dock leaves,
a sly fox crept up and snatched her in his mouth!

Before she had time to quack he was heading
for his lair. But Cindy had been watching.
Without hesitating she rushed after the fox and
caught the tip of his long tail in her sharp beak.

As the fox spun round, she pecked him hard on the nose. His mouth dropped open and Daisy fell out. Now he was really mad and rushed at them. But Mrs Duck and Mrs Swan flew at him hissing furiously and off he ran. Daisy couldn't thank them enough. "That's what friends are for!" said Cindy. And Mrs Swan and Mrs Duck, who were the best of friends, could not agree more.

LIKE A DUCK TO WATER

Mrs Duck swam proudly across the farm pond
followed by a line of fluffy ducklings. Hidden in
the safety of the nest Dozy Duckling peeked
out and watched them go. He wished he was
brave enough to go with them but he was afraid
of the water! Instead, he pretended to be asleep,
and Mrs Duck told the others to leave him alone.

When they returned that night they told him tales of all the scary animals they had met by the pond. "There's a big thing with hot breath called Horse," said Dotty. "There's a huge smelly pink thing called Pig," said Dickie. "But

worst of all," said Doris, "there's a great grey bird, called Heron. Pig says he gobbles up little ducklings for breakfast!"
At that all the little ducklings squawked with fear and excitement.

Next morning, Mrs Duck hurried the ducklings out for their morning parade. Dozy kept his eyes shut until they had gone then looked up to see a great grey bird towering over him! He leapt into the water crying, "Help, wait for me!" But the others started laughing! "It's a trick! Heron won't eat you. We just wanted you to come swimming. And you've taken to it like a duck to water!"

LITTLEST PIGLET

Littlest Piglet had so many brothers and sisters
that he was always the last to get anything to eat.

The others were all bigger, louder and
pushier than he was.

"I hate being the littlest," he said to his mummy.

"But you're my special little piglet!" said his
mummy. But somehow he didn't
feel special at all.

One day the farmer let the piglets out into the yard while he went to the market. But a big storm blew up. The wind whistled round Littlest Piglet's ears and made him shiver and then the rain began to fall.

But worst of all, the wind caught the barn door and banged it shut! Now all the piglets were stuck outside and who knew when the farmer would get back!

Proudly he pushed open the door and
everyone ran in, safe from the storm.
"Oh, thank you," they cried. "You're a hero!
You can have first turn at the
feeding trough tonight!"

Littlest Piglet snuggled up happily in the smallest, warmest space next to his mummy. "Didn't I say you were special?" she said, and Littlest Piglet smiled.

The little piglets ran off squealing and chasing – through the apple trees in the orchard, past the sheep in the meadow, until they stopped for a rest, puffing and panting, by the stream. They had been having so much fun, they had quite forgotten to look where they were going.

Then Smallest Piglet said, " I'm hungry! Can we go home for lunch now?" Biggest Piglet looked around him. His ears drooped. "I can't remember the way. Can any of you?" The others all shook their heads, miserably.

Then Clever Piglet spoke up.

"Just follow the acorns," he said.

"What acorns?" cried all the little piglets.

"The acorns I left behind along the way," he said.

"Well, you really are a CLEVER piglet, Clever Piglet!" said Biggest Piglet, smiling happily.

And they followed the acorns all the way home.

GREEDY PIGLET

All the farm animals were busy getting ready for the barn dance. All, that is, except Greedy Piglet. The air was full of the most delicious smells of pumpkin pies and corn. Greedy Piglet couldn't help himself; he took a pie and hid under the table with it. And when he had finished that he took some sweet juicy corn and gobbled that up too. "It's meant for the barn dance!" the others scolded him.

But Greedy Piglet couldn't wait. He gathered together a whole pile of cakes and buns, and sneaked into a quiet corner. He ate so much that his tummy was round as a barrel. All that eating made him sleepy. Soon he was curled up, fast asleep.

As the greedy little piglet slept on, night fell and the stars began to twinkle in the sky. The farm animals gathered, and the barn dance began. Cockerel brought a fiddle and everyone danced as Greedy Piglet snored on.

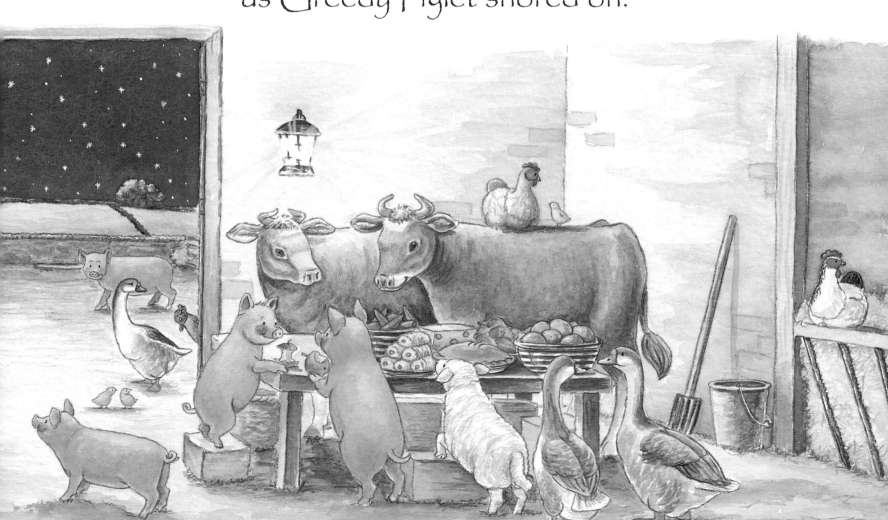

Suddenly, Greedy Piglet woke up with a jump.
He could hear the sound of a fiddle playing.
"Have I missed the food?" he cried, looking around in
dismay. His tummy gave a loud rumble!
"All the food has gone, Greedy Piglet!" everyone
laughed. "But come and join the dancing." So Greedy
Piglet danced under the stars until dawn.

BEST PIGLET

All the piglets were excited. There was to be a competition for Best Piglet and everyone wanted to win...except for Scruffy Piglet, who liked being messy, and just loved to play. But the others were too busy. "Keep out of the way, Scruffy," the piglets fussed, as they bathed and brushed themselves, and polished their hooves. Soon they were spotless and gleaming. All they had to do was stay that way!

Competition

prize for

Best Piglet

Scruffy Piglet rolled in the straw, giggling and playing until it was time for the competition to begin. As the other piglets lined up for inspection, Scruffy Piglet took a place at the end of the line. The judge was a stern looking sheep dog.

He looked along the row of neat, polished piglets until he came to Scruffy Piglet at the end. He couldn't believe his eyes! Scruffy Piglet was the scruffiest little piglet he had ever seen! He was just about to say so when a great commotion broke out.

Suddenly there were chickens running and flapping and clucking, and the piglets scarpered in all directions, bumping into one another and falling in the mud. Scruffy Piglet sat watching, chuckling to himself. By the time they all lined up again, the judge was not impressed. "You are the muddiest piglets I ever saw!" he scolded. "I have no choice than to name Scruffy — Best Piglet!"

Which made Scruffy laugh till he cried!

LITTLE CHICK LOST

"Stay close, Little Chick!" said Mummy, as they set out to visit Mrs Duck, who lived on the pond. Little Chick tried to keep up with Mummy, but there were so many interesting things to look at that he soon got lost in the long grass.

He was busy watching a shiny beetle climb a stem of grass, when a dark shadow fell over him. Little Chick looked up to see a huge dribbling mouth coming towards him!

It was a hungry fox! "Help!" he cried, looking around for somewhere to hide.

Just then, Spot, the farm dog, appeared and

with a great woof he chased the fox away.

He was good at protecting the farm animals.

Mummy arrived flapping her wings.

"I told you to stay close," she said, tucking

Little Chick under her wing. And from then on,

that is just where Little Chick stayed!

THE DISAPPEARING EGGS

Mrs Hen had been sitting on her nest for
a long time, and she was tired and uncomfortable.
"I wish these eggs would hurry up and hatch!"
she said to herself, crossly. But all she could do
was sit and wait, so she closed her eyes
and soon fell fast asleep.

She dreamt she was sitting on her nest when
all of a sudden it started to wobble and shake.
She was tipped this way, and that, being
poked and prodded as the eggs moved
beneath her - someone was stealing her eggs!
A deep voice was saying,
"What lovely big ones!" It must be Mr Fox!
She had to save her eggs!

Mrs Hen woke with a start, and looked down at her nest in alarm. Sure enough, her eggs had disappeared - but in their place were six fluffy chicks, all prodding her with their sharp little beaks.

"What lovely big ones!" said a deep voice
nearby. It was Old Ned, the donkey.
"Aren't they just!" said Mrs Hen with relief.
"They were certainly worth the wait!"

MAKING A SPLASH!

One day, Mrs Hen and her chicks were walking near the pond when Mrs Duck swam by, followed by a line of ducklings. The ducklings splashed around ducking and diving in the water. "Can we play in the water too?" the chicks asked Mrs Hen. "It looks like fun!"

"Oh, no, dears," said Mrs Hen. "Chicks and water don't mix!" This made the chicks very miserable. "It's not fair!" they grumbled. "We wish we were ducklings!"

On the way home, a big black cloud appeared and it started to rain. Soon the chicks' fluffy feathers were wet through.

They scurried back to the henhouse as fast as they could and arrived wet, cold and shivering. Soon they were snuggled in the cosy warm straw, and their feathers were dry and fluffy again.

"Imagine being wet all the time!" said the chicks. "Thank goodness we're not ducklings, after all!"

CHEEKY CHICK

Cheeky Chick was a playful little chick. He was always playing tricks on his brothers and sisters. He would hide in the long grass, then jump out on them in surprise, shouting, "Boo!" One day they decided to get their own back. "Let's play hide and seek," they said.

They left Cheeky Chick to count to ten,
while they all went to hide. Cheeky Chick
hunted high and low for his brothers
and sisters. He looked in all his favourite

hiding places but they were nowhere to be found. "Come out," he called. "I give up!" But no one came.

So Cheeky Chick carried on looking.
He searched carefully all through the farmyard,
through the vegetable patch and along the
hedgerow at the edge of the field. He even
looked in the haystack, which took a very long
time, but there was no sign of his brothers and
sisters to be found amongst the hay.

By now it was getting dark, and Cheeky

Chick was feeling scared and lonely.

"It's no use," he said to himself. "I'll have

to go home." He hurried to the henhouse

and opened the door. "Surprise!" came

a loud chorus. His brothers and sisters

had been hiding there all along! It was

a long time before Cheeky Chick played

tricks on them again.